Spellb♥und Ponies

Rainbows and Ribbons

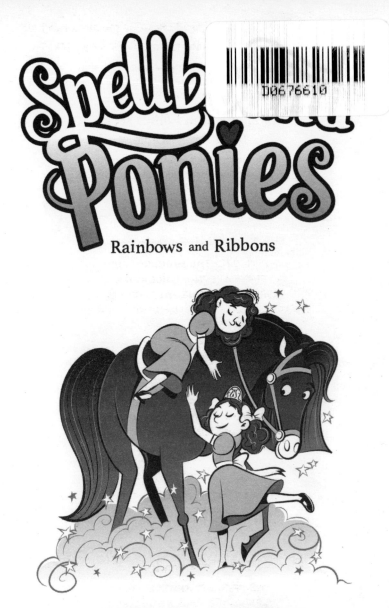

STACY GREGG

HarperCollins *Children's Books*

First published in Great Britain by
HarperCollins *Children's Books* in 2021
HarperCollins *Children's Books* is a division of HarperCollins*Publishers* Ltd
1 London Bridge Street
London SE1 9GF

www.harpercollins.co.uk

HarperCollins*Publishers*
1st Floor, Watermarque Building, Ringsend Road
Dublin 4, Ireland

1

Text copyright © Stacy Gregg 2021
Illustrations copyright © Crush Creative 2021
Cover illustrations copyright © Crush Creative 2021
Cover design copyright © HarperCollins*Publishers* Ltd 2021
All rights reserved

ISBN 978-0-00-840299-0

Stacy Gregg and Crush Creative assert the moral right to be
identified as the author and illustrator of the work respectfully.

A CIP catalogue record for this title is available from the British Library.

Typeset in Cambria 12/24pt by
Palimpsest Book Production Ltd, Falkirk, Stirlingshire
Printed and bound in the UK using 100% renewable electricity
at CPI Group (UK) Ltd

Conditions of Sale
This book is sold subject to the condition that it shall not, by way of
trade or otherwise, be lent, re-sold, hired out or otherwise circulated
without the publisher's prior consent in any form, binding or cover other
than that in which it is published and without a similar condition including
this condition being imposed on the subsequent purchaser.

MIX
**Paper from
responsible sources**
FSC™ C007454

This book is produced from independently certified FSC™ paper
to ensure responsible forest management.

For more information visit: www.harpercollins.co.uk/green

Chapter One

At the breakfast table in Pemberley Cottage, Olivia's big sister Ella was in a very grumpy mood.

'It's a Saturday and I'm so bored! I wish we'd never moved to this stupid, tiny village in the middle of nowhere,' Ella grizzled. 'There's never anything to do.'

'Someone got out of bed on the wrong side this morning!' Mrs Campbell arched an eyebrow.

'I got up from the same side I always do!' Ella snapped. 'There's a wall on the other side.'

'Look, why don't you spend the day down at Pemberley Stables with Olivia?' Mrs Campbell suggested. 'That might cheer you up, and you two never play together these days.'

'No! Ella can't come with me!' Olivia blurted out before she could stop herself.

Olivia could have sworn she saw a look of hurt flash across Ella's face, and that made her feel bad, but she didn't want her sister going to the stables – not when there was another Spellbound pony about to be rescued.

'Bah!' Ella grouched. 'As if I'd want to play imaginary games with you at your stupid old spooky stables anyway! I'm going to hang out in my room.'

Mrs Campbell sighed as she watched her eldest daughter stomp off. 'Is it just me or is she extra grumpy today?'

'Definitely extra!' Olivia agreed.

Olivia, on the other hand, was in an especially cheery mood as she raced out of the door and headed for the stables. It was always a good day

when a new Spellbound pony was about to arrive
and an adventure lay ahead. There was a skip in
Olivia's step as she made her way down the
country lanes and along the pebbled driveway to
the entrance of the long-abandoned stables.

'Eliza?' she whispered as she slid open the front
door. 'Are you here? It's me!'

It was impossible to see anything in the gloom.
And then out of the darkness Olivia spied two
amber eyes blinking back at her.

'Eliza? Why aren't you speaking? Hey, wait!
You're not—'

Suddenly, there was a fearsome flutter of
feathers and beating of wings, and the next thing
Olivia knew the glowing amber eyes were coming
straight at her!

'Yikes!' Olivia shrieked, shutting her eyes tightly
as the hoot owl swooped above her. When she

opened them again, the owl had flown outside to perch on top of the ivy above the stable door.

'You've got your feathers in a flap today, haven't you?' Olivia growled at the bird. The owl blinked back at her as if to say, *Well, it's your fault for waking me up!*

It was a strange coincidence, Olivia thought, that the owl had chosen to perch on that exact spot. Ignoring his bad-tempered glare, she reached up to the ivy and pushed the leaves aside so that she could read the words that lay hidden underneath, carved into the stone of the wall.

The deepest magic binds these stables
Unless two brave girls can turn the tables.
The curse on each horse must be found,
Then break their spell to be unbound.

Olivia remembered the first time she had read the words on the wall. She had asked Eliza if it was a poem but Eliza had explained that it was more like a witch's spell – and rather a good one – that had put a curse on the stables and trapped the ponies in time.

Olivia and Eliza had become best friends as they attempted one by one to break the spells that were making the ponies naughty. Together they had already set four of the Spellbound ponies free. And today Olivia had arrived to help Eliza summon pony number five.

'Don't worry about the owl. He's in a frightful grump today.'

Another pair of eyes, these ones as brilliant green as emeralds, glowed from inside the darkened stables. Then, a moment later, Eliza appeared in the sunshine. She wore her tousled red curls tied up in a messy ponytail and she was dressed in her white Georgian nightgown. Eliza looked to be about the same age as Olivia, which was nine, but in fact she was actually *two hundred and nine* due to being a ghost!

Olivia, who'd been fooled before, had to resist the urge to give her bestie a big hug, knowing that her arms would swish right through Eliza as if she were made of mist.

'We've got a visitor,' Eliza said brightly.

'I know,' Olivia groaned. 'He nearly hit me in the head flying out of the doorway!'

'No, no,' Eliza said, 'not the owl. Look – on the plaque on the stall door. I can see the letters of a pony's name beginning to glow. All we need to do is say the name out loud as we step across the threshold of the stall, and the pony will appear!'

'Oh, you're right!' Olivia was excited to see the brass plaque on the door glowing with the name shimmering upon it. 'A new pony is here!'

'Time for us to get summoning, then,' Eliza said. 'Are you ready?'

'Absolutely!' Olivia took a deep breath and as the girls stepped over the threshold together she invoked the witch's spell by speaking the Spellbound pony's name out loud.

'Gus!'

The very second the Spellbound pony's name was spoken, the stall began to fill with mystical mist. It rose up through the straw on the floor in tendrils, drifting up and up, until soon it had filled the whole stall.

'I can't see a thing!' Olivia said.

'Me neither!' Eliza replied.

'You think you've got problems?' another voice moaned through the fog. **'It's much worse for me! Enchanted mist plays havoc with my asthma, you know! Oh, and it feels all clammy against my fetlocks! Just my rotten luck!'**

'Oh, hello!' Olivia said. 'There's a pony in here!'

The mist cleared and the girls could see the summoning had indeed worked. Standing in the stall beside Olivia and Eliza was a very handsome pony with a wonderful, lush black mane and tail and a rich, russet-brown coat.

'Oooh, hooray, he's a bay! My very favourite colour for a horse,' Olivia exclaimed.

 17

'Humph!' The pony pulled a face. '**I doubt that very much! Now, if you had said your favourite colour was grey or even palomino, I might believe you. Those are stylish colours for a pony. Bay is boring! Just my rotten luck to be a bay, I say.**'

'Er . . .' Olivia was taken aback. 'No, truly, it is my very fave colour! And it really is lovely to meet you. You must be Gus?'

'**Yes. Not much of a name, is it?**' The bay pony sighed. '**Why, oh, why couldn't they have named me something dashing like Prancer? Or a swashbuckling kind of name like Pegasus or Jet?**'

'Would you like me to call you Jet?' Olivia offered. 'I could, if that's what you want?'

'**Oh, don't try to humour me!**' Gus grizzled. '**It's far too late for that. I'm already in a very bad mood.**'

And to prove it, he did what ponies always do

when they are moody and put his ears flat back against his head.

'Gosh!' Eliza pulled away in shock. 'He really is grumpy, isn't he?'

'He certainly is,' Olivia agreed. 'Eliza, I think we might just have found out what mischief the witch's spell has caused this time. Poor Gus! It looks like he's been cursed to be grumpy!'

Chapter Two

'Humph! Don't think you can just stand there and talk about me like I'm not even here!' Gus said grouchily. 'I can hear everything you say, you know! Which is typical. Just my rotten luck. Here I am, a talking pony, and no one even wants to speak to me!'

'Dear me!' Eliza shook her head. 'He really is very grumpy, isn't he? How do you go about un-grumping a pony?'

'We'll have to try to cheer him up somehow,' Olivia said. 'How about it, Gus? What would improve your mood? Do you like food?'

'Humph! What kind of food?' Gus grumbled.

'An ice cream, perhaps?' Olivia suggested.

'Ick! No! Too cold on my tongue!' Gus griped.

'Fair enough,' Olivia said. 'Perhaps a slice of pizza, then?'

'Holding the crust makes my hooves greasy,' Gus sniffed.

'Lollies?' Eliza suggested. 'Or perhaps a sugar cube? Ponies always love sugar.'

'Oh, how can you even suggest such a thing?' Gus groaned. 'My poor teeth are aching at the very thought of it!'

'Right.' Olivia gritted her own teeth now. 'So food is off the menu. How about fun and games?'

'Oh, how I loathe fun,' Gus sighed. 'And games? Even worse!'

'No more fun and games, then,' Olivia said. 'Gotcha.'

'What else can we do?' Eliza wondered. 'There must be something that makes a pony happy.'

'Oooh, I know!' Olivia clapped her hands in delight. 'How about we go for a ride, Gus? Why don't I take you for a lovely hack?'

Gus sighed even more heavily. **'All right, then,'** he said, **'but I won't like it.'**

'That's the spirit!' Olivia said, putting on the biggest smile she could muster as she hastily grabbed Gus's saddle and bridle and threw them on before he could change his mind.

'Where shall we go?' she asked.

'Somewhere ghastly, I expect,' Gus muttered.

'I know just the place!' Eliza said.

And at that moment the stall began to fill with enchanted mist once more.

'Oh no!' Gus groaned. **'Here we go again! I'll be needing my inhaler if this keeps up . . .'**

When the mist cleared this time, they were in a very pretty forest. Dappled light filtered through the leaves of the trees on to an elegant lake where swans were gliding between bulrushes. The lake was bordered by wild flowers, and running like a ribbon through this pleasant scene was a bridle path.

'Oh, it's so beautiful!' Olivia gasped.

'Yes, and this bridle path winds all the way round the Pemberley lake,' Eliza said. 'I came here often with Chessie before I became a ghost.'

'It's all right, I suppose, if you like that sort of thing,' Gus sniffed, **'although the wild flowers will give me hay fever, I expect. Just my rotten luck.'**

'All the same,' Olivia said, 'let's press on and try to make the best of it, shall we, Gus?'

She mounted up on to Gus's back. 'Off we go, then!' she clucked.

'Oww!' Gus squawked.

'What's wrong?' Olivia asked.

'I trod on a stone,' Gus grumped. 'Argh!'

'And what now?' Olivia asked.

'There's a gnat in my ear,' Gus said.

'There – it's gone. Better now?' Eliza asked.

'No. I can still hear buzzing,' Gus complained. 'Probably the honeybees on the wild flowers. They're so annoying with their smug bzzz bzzz . . . and the birds too! They're almost worse than the bees with their ridiculous tweeting. Why does all this . . . nature . . . have to be here? Just my rotten luck!'

'I think we should give up and go home now,' Olivia sighed.

'I think you're right,' Eliza agreed. 'He's hopeless. Oh, wait a moment! Who is that riding towards us on the bridle path?'

Up ahead of the girls, sitting astride an elegant grey mare, was a woman in a silver gown with a diamond tiara on her head.

'It's the Duchess of Derryshire!' Olivia said. 'Hello, Duchess.'

'Oh, what a coincidence,' the duchess trilled.
'You two are just the girls I was looking for!'

'We are?' Olivia said.

'Yes, indeed,' the duchess replied. 'Did you
know it is the twins' birthday in just three days?
The girls are turning eight and I'm planning an
enormous surprise party. That's when I thought
of you two. You see, a Spellbound pony is just
what I need! The twins are desperately keen to
have pony rides and what could be more special
than having a talking pony at their party? Why,
this must be your new pony here. What's your
name?'

'You can call me Gus,' Gus groaned, **'if you
must!'**

'Splendid!' the duchess said. 'He's just the ticket.
Olivia and Eliza, you simply must bring Gus to the
party. Oh, the girls will be *so* thrilled!'

Olivia looked nervously at Eliza.

'Umm . . . the thing is, your duchessness, Gus might not be suitable for pony rides.'

'Oh, I'm sure he'll be fine,' the duchess insisted. 'So that's all settled, then! I'll see you and your Spellbound pony at the party. How marvellous of you to agree to this!'

Before the girls could say another word, the duchess had disappeared in a swirl of enchanted mist.

'Did we say yes?' Olivia boggled. 'I missed the bit where we said yes!'

'I don't think anyone ever says no to the duchess.' Eliza rolled her eyes.

Olivia gave a heavy sigh. 'Right. Well, I think we'll be off home, then.'

'Livvy? Are you okay?' Eliza asked.

'Not really,' Olivia replied. 'I'd been hoping I

could put Gus in a good mood but I think his bad mood has worn me down. I've come over all gloomy myself. Shall we go now?'

With a weary trudge, Olivia headed back out of the stable and into the yard.

'Don't be sad,' Eliza implored as she watched her best friend depart. 'Look, why don't you give Bess, Prince, Sparkle and Champ carrots before you go home?'

'All right, then,' Olivia sighed. But even as she fed the ponies their treats she couldn't shake off her miserable mood, and by the time she left for home she was feeling very glum indeed. Had they finally met a Spellbound pony that was impossible to save?

Chapter Three

At the dinner table that evening, Olivia felt so miserable she could barely bring herself to lift her fork to her mouth.

'Not hungry, sweetie?' Mrs Campbell asked.

'Not really,' Olivia sighed. 'It's been a tough day.'

'You could eat a few of your vegetables at least,' her mum said.

Olivia frowned and prodded at her plate. 'Yuck.

Why do we have to have broccoli? It's like eating trees.'

'Try some peas, then?' her mum suggested.

'They're worse,' said Olivia, squishing the peas meanly with her fork. 'Too tiny and too green.'

Mrs Campbell sighed. 'Honestly, Olivia, what is up? Ella can be grumpy at times, but it's very out of character for you. You're always such a ray of sunshine!'

'I'm just not feeling very sunny, Mum,' Olivia said glumly.

'You must be overtired,' Mrs Campbell said. 'A good night's sleep will sort you out.'

'Wowsers!' Olivia dropped her cutlery and stared at her mum. 'Would that work, do you think?'

'I expect so,' Mrs Campbell replied. 'There's

nothing like a nap to improve the mood.'

'Thanks, Mum! You're brilliant!' Olivia cheered

up enormously and began to tuck into the broccoli.

'Am I?' said Mrs Campbell. 'Well, in that case,

there's ice cream for dessert . . .'

Olivia could hardly wait to get to the stables the next morning and tell Eliza everything.

'Firstly,' she said, 'I suspect that bad moods might in fact be infectious.'

'Really?' Eliza was astonished. 'Gosh, do you really think that we could catch being grumpy off Gus, a bit like catching a cold?'

'Exactly like that!' Olivia said. 'You see, I'm usually in a very good mood but yesterday, after being with Gus, I found myself utterly miserable.'

'Hmmmm. We shall have to be careful, then,' Eliza said. 'Perhaps we shouldn't get too close to him?'

'Or perhaps we can combat catching his grumps by being extra cheery ourselves?' Olivia suggested. 'Then he'll be infected with *our* good humour instead.'

'Yes,' Eliza agreed, 'let's try it.'

'There's something else as well,' Olivia said. 'My mum says a decent sleep improves a bad mood. Eliza, we need to convince Gus to take a good long nap. That may cure him entirely!'

'A nap, you say?' Eliza mused. 'So he could be bad-tempered because he's tired?'

'Exactly!' Olivia said. She slung the big sack that she'd brought along with her back on to her shoulder. 'I have some things in here that might help. Let's go and see Gus.'

Gus had added a new sign to his stall overnight. It was painted with big black letters that read:

'I don't think he wants visitors,' Eliza said.

'It's the curse, not him,' Olivia said, ignoring the sign and opening the door. 'I'm going in.'

Gus was lying on the straw in a sulk. **'Hey!'** he raised his head and put his ears back. **'I put a sign up! Can't you read?'**

'Oh, did you?' Olivia replied. 'Well, never mind, I'm here now, Gus and I have some presents in this sack for you.'

'Presents, eh?' Gus's ears pricked forward. **'I suppose it wouldn't hurt to take a look.'**

Olivia opened the sack. 'Look!' She smiled. 'A soft, snuggly blanket.'

Gus's ears went back once more. **'I don't have any use for a snuggly blanket.'**

'All the same, why don't you try it on?' Eliza suggested.

'Oh, but I hate trying things on,' Gus grumbled

as he sank further into the straw on the floor.
Olivia rushed forward and tucked the snuggly
blanket round him.

'Feeling sleepy?' she asked.

'Not at all,' Gus replied stubbornly.

'Well, perhaps you'll feel like a nap after this . . .'
Olivia dug around in the sack once more and pulled
out a Thermos flask and a mug. 'Warm milk with
honey,' she said. 'It's perfect to make a pony dozy.'

'I don't know,' Gus moaned as she poured him
a cup. **'I might be lactose-intolerant.'**

'Oh, you're intolerant all right,' Olivia agreed,
'but try it anyway.'

Gus sipped away at the mug of warm milk while
Olivia pulled more items out of the sack.

'How do you like that lovely, soft pillow, then?'
Olivia asked as she propped it under Gus's head.

'It's too squishy and . . .' Gus began to

complain but then he stopped and gave a loud yawn.

Olivia looked across at her friend and gave her a wink.

'He yawned!' Eliza whispered. 'It must be working! He's getting sleepy. What else have you got in there?'

'Something everybody needs to get a good night's sleep,' Olivia said. 'I had to borrow this one.' With a flourish, she produced a teddy bear.

'Oh, it's Raymond!' Eliza recognised the soft toy that belonged to Bess, their first Spellbound pony.

'Yes, it was very kind of her to lend him to us,' Olivia said as she passed the teddy to Gus, who was now looking very sleepy indeed.

'Quick!' Eliza whispered. 'He's almost nodded off. Time for the lullaby!'

'*Rock-a-bye, Gussie, on the treetop . . .*' Olivia began.

'*When the pony sleeps the grumping will stop,*' Eliza continued.

'**Humpf!, wumpf . . .**' Gus began to mutter, and then the muttering became a soft, gentle drone . . . and soon he was wheezing contentedly.

'He's snoring!' Eliza said excitedly. 'We did it! He's asleep!'

'Shush.' Olivia placed a finger to her lips. 'Let's sneak out and leave him to nap.'

The two girls backed away from the sleeping pony and slipped outside the stall.

'What now?' Eliza asked.

Olivia shrugged. 'I guess we wait,' she said.

Time ticked by.

'That nap is going on a very long time!' Eliza said. 'It's been almost three hours!'

'But just think what a brilliant mood he'll be in after all that lovely sleep,' Olivia said.

'Oh, listen, I think he's waking up!' Eliza said as they heard a stirring from within the stall. 'Shall we go and see what kind of mood he's in?'

'I don't think we need to go in to find out,' Olivia said. 'Look!'

Raymond the teddy came flying through the air out of Gus's stall, followed quickly by the mug, the snuggly blanket and the squishy pillow. And then Gus stuck his head over the stall door.

'Yikes!' Eliza said. 'His ears are flattened back further than ever before!'

'Bah! Who made me go to bed?' Gus grumped. **'Sleeping like a baby is for babies!'**

'Oh dear,' Eliza said. 'He's woken up on the wrong side of the bed, hasn't he?'

'A witch's curse is obviously too powerful to be defeated by a long snooze,' Eliza sighed.

'Well, we'll just have to find another cure – and

quickly,' Olivia said. 'The birthday party for the twins is looming!'

'Isn't it a coincidence,' Eliza mused, 'how they both have their birthday on the same day?'

Olivia boggled at her friend. 'You are joking, aren't you, Eliza?'

'Joking?' Eliza said. 'Hmmm. I'm pretty sure I *wasn't* trying to be funny.'

'Oh!' Olivia felt the light bulb above her head switch on. And something else was becoming clear to Olivia too. 'I've just had the most brilliant idea. I know how we can cure Gus of his grumps!'

'Oh, yay!' Eliza clapped her hands with glee. 'How? Tell me!'

'I'll do better than that. Meet me back here tonight and I'll show you!' Olivia's eyes were shining. She was certain that her plan would work this time.

Chapter Four

When Olivia arrived back at the stables that evening, the owl was sitting on the ivy above the plaque once more. His round amber eyes shone like golden moons in the darkness as he peered down at her.

'Hey, you!' Olivia said.

'Whoooo,' the owl replied.

'What do you call an owl dressed in a suit

of armour?' Olivia asked.

The owl looked perplexed.

'A knight owl!' Olivia said.

'Gosh! That's very funny!' Eliza giggled,

appearing from nowhere right beside her.

'Yikes!' Olivia spun round in shock. 'How many times have I told you not to sneak up on me like that? You totally made me jump!'

'Sorry,' Eliza said. 'Sneaking up is just what ghosts do, though. That was an excellent joke! Did you just make it up on the spot?'

'No,' Olivia confessed. 'I read it in a book I've been studying.'

'Studying jokes?' Eliza said. 'Why would you do that?'

'To brighten up Gus!' Olivia said as she strode ahead into the stables. 'I've got a plan to make him laugh. After all, you can't stay grumpy when you're laughing, can you?'

'True, true!' Eliza agreed. 'They do say laughter is the best medicine, so perhaps it will cure him.'

'Look.' Olivia showed Eliza a page of paper with notes scribbled all over it. 'I've written down loads of jokes to tell him. All we need is the right sort of atmosphere to put Gus in the mood for a giggle.'

'Oooh! I know just the place!' Eliza enthused. 'Come on, let's go!'

When the girls entered Gus's stall the pony was lying on the floor staring blankly at the wall.

'What on earth are you doing, Gus?' Olivia asked.

Gus rolled over and groaned. **'I'm being miserable – obviously.'**

'Well, stop it!' Eliza said firmly. 'Pull yourself together and get up . . . we're going out!'

At these words, the enchanted mist began once more to rise up through the straw on the stable floor.

'Oh no!' Gus groaned. **'Not again! I shall get tuberculosis at this rate . . .'**

But the Spellbound pony's sour complaints
were drowned out by the haunting sound
of laughter, and then the mist cleared and
Gus and the girls found themselves in a dark
cabaret club filled with men and women in

glamorous evening clothes, all sitting at little tables.

On the stage in front of the audience a woman was performing a dance with feathered fans while reciting poems.

'That's Lillie Lollipop the famous entertainer, and very funny she is too,' Eliza explained.

Meanwhile, Lillie Lollipop had noticed the new arrivals in her audience. 'Well, fancy that! Visitors!' She gestured for the spotlight to be turned on to Olivia, Eliza and Gus, and the crowd stared.

'And, my goodness, one of them is a horse! Hey, you there, my friend! Why the long face?'

There were hoots of laughter from the crowd at this.

'I don't get it,' Gus, said flatly. **'I do have a long face but why are they all laughing?'**

'Because it's a joke,' Olivia explained. 'Come and sit down, Gus, and watch the show.'

As they moved between the tables Lillie finished up her performance. She bowed as the crowd threw roses as a tribute, and she gathered them up.

With a farewell wave, she disappeared behind the velvet curtains.

'Quick!' Eliza hissed to Olivia. 'Before everyone leaves. This is your chance. Take the stage – get up there!'

'I don't know,' Olivia murmured. 'Now that I'm here, it seems very scary.'

'But you have to!' Eliza insisted. 'Remember? We need to make Gus laugh if we're going to break the witch's spell.'

'Okay,' Olivia said. 'I'll do it.'

'Break a leg,' Eliza said encouragingly.

'No, don't, Livvy!' Gus said. **'You'll be on crutches for months!'**

'I don't really want her to break a leg. It's a showbiz phrase,' Eliza reassured him. 'It means *good luck*.'

'Well, why don't you just say good luck, then?' Gus moaned.

Olivia, meanwhile, had made her way on to the stage, and now the spotlight and the crowd's attention was entirely upon her. Olivia's heart was racing as she managed to squeak, 'Good evening, ladies and gentlemen. My name is Olivia and I'm here with my friend Gus who, as you can see, is a pony. I'm hoping tonight we can make him laugh, so here goes . . .'

Olivia pulled her written page of jokes out of her pocket.

'What did the horse say when it fell over?'

The audience went quiet.

'I can't giddy-up!' Olivia said.

There was a groan from the crowd.

'They aren't laughing,' Gus said to Eliza. **'Not surprising, really. Horses falling over isn't funny!'**

'Shhhh, Gus,' Eliza whispered. 'Give Livvy a chance!'

Olivia was sweating now and her hands were shaking as she read further down the page.

'Where do horses go when they're sick?' Olivia said. 'They go to horse-pital!'

In the audience there was a ripple of laughter at this one.

'Hmmm, I don't get it,' Gus grumped. 'There's absolutely nothing funny about a sick horse. In fact, I'm beginning to wonder if Livvy isn't a bit of a meanie?'

Olivia cleared her throat and read out the next joke. 'Which horses like to go out after dark? Night-mares!'

There was laughter from the audience . . . but Gus was not amused.

'Boo! Hiss!' the Spellbound pony heckled. 'Your so-called jokes are not funny at all – and I'm off!'

With a stomp of his hooves, he stood up and stormed out of the club.

'So much for comedy,' Eliza sighed.

'I was really awful, wasn't I,' Olivia agreed as

they made their way back to Spellbound Stables that evening.

'Only as far as Gus was concerned!' Eliza said. 'The rest of the audience loved you. In fact, they asked me if I was your manager. They want to book you to perform next week—'

'Oh, hullo!' Livvy interrupted her. 'Look, it's the Duchess of Derryshire. She's at Gus's stall waiting for us. I wonder what she wants.'

The duchess was looking very impatient as she paced back and forth on the doorstep beside Gus.

'Ah, girls!' she said. 'About time. I just dropped by to give you the pony's costume for tomorrow.'

'Tomorrow?' Olivia said.

'Yes – tomorrow!' The duchess looked cross. 'It's the twins' birthday party. Surely you haven't forgotten?'

'No, no, of course not, Duchess,' Eliza reassured her. 'It's just that it sneaked up on us. Doesn't time fly when you're having fun!'

'Does it?' Gus groaned. **'I wouldn't know.'**

'Anyway –' said the duchess, ignoring him – 'here it is. I'll expect him to be wearing it *tomorrow*.'

She handed the costume to Olivia. It was made of rainbow-coloured silk in brilliant stripes.

'Gosh, it's very cheerful, isn't it?' Olivia said.

'Yes, well, birthdays are very happy occasions,' the duchess agreed. 'Anyway, I'm off to organise the cake and balloons. I'll see you girls and Gus *tomorrow*. Three p.m. sharp and don't forget!'

She disappeared through the door on a gust of enchanted mist. Gus skulked inside his stall and collapsed on to the straw with a dramatic moan.

'What a miserable night it's been,' he whinged. **'I'd like to be left alone now to sulk, if you don't mind.'**

'Well, I've had enough for one night too,' Olivia agreed. 'You go and sulk, Gus, and I'm going to head for bed myself.'

'But you'll come back in the morning, won't you?' Eliza looked concerned. 'I know it's going to take a miracle to make Gus happy in time for the birthday party but we must keep trying. Two brave girls together, remember, Livvy?'

'Oh, don't worry, I'll be back,' Olivia reassured her best friend. 'No matter how impossible it seems, we'll do everything in our power to cheer Gus up and break the spell.'

* ★ *

As Olivia left for home that night, she closed the stable door behind her, but the moment she was gone, Horace the Hunt Master came tiptoeing through the shadows. Horace haunted the stables and made mischief of one sort or another to keep the ponies trapped by the witch's spell.

Now, as he slunk down the corridor, head wobbling like mad, he was whistling a merry tune.

'Gus, my good fellow,' he chortled as he opened the door to the grumpy pony's stall, 'you look gloomy.'

'I have a long face,' Gus grumbled.

'Quite right!' Horace said. 'Don't laugh at anything – the last thing we need is for you to cheer up. That would break the spell. That's not why I'm here at all.'

'Then why are you here?' Gus groaned. **'Just my rotten luck to have company when I'm about to go to sleep.'**

'Oh, you are in a foul mood!' Horace chuckled. 'Good old grumpy Gus. I've only come to help you.'

'Help me?' Gus said. **'How?'**

'Oh, you'll see!' With that Horace produced a

pair of scissors. His busy blades swished in the moonlight as he chopped away at Gus's costume, chortling with glee. 'You're going to be the life and soul of the party, my glum chum; you're going to give them all a birthday surprise they'll never forget!'

Chapter Five

On the morning of the party, Olivia arrived bright and early at Pemberley Stables and found Eliza pacing up and down outside Gus's stall.

'Thank goodness you're here!' Eliza exclaimed. 'There's been a problem with Gus's costume!'

'Doesn't it fit?' Olivia asked.

'Oh, it's much worse than that,' Eliza said. 'Look!'

Olivia opened the door to Gus's stall and found the pony in his rainbow suit – except the rainbows had been shredded to ribbons!

'Oh no! Gus! What have you done?'

'I knew it looked bad,' Gus groaned. **'Just my rotten luck. I should never have listened when Horace said he wanted to make a few alterations.'**

'Horace!' Olivia shrieked.

'Oooh, I hear my name!' came a chortle from the corridor. 'The girls must be here admiring my handiwork!'

Olivia and Eliza spun round to see the gloating grin of the Hunt Master.

'Horace, you're an utter party pooper! You've ruined Gus's costume!' Olivia fumed.

'Indeed!' Horace said gleefully. 'With no costume to cheer up the kiddies, it's going to be an utterly miserable party, isn't it, Gus?'

63

'Horace spent all of last night telling me what dreadful occasions birthdays are!' Gus grumped. 'Livvy, did you know they put candles on the cake? Madness! I could easily burn my tongue!'

'You blow the candles out before you eat the cake,' Olivia sighed.

'And here's the most unbelievable bit,' Gus continued grumbling. 'Apparently there are all these lovely presents but then one greedy person snatches them all up for themselves!'

'They *snatch* the presents because it's *their* birthday!' Eliza said in exasperation.

'Humph! It all still sounds a bit unfair, if you ask me!' Gus muttered. 'Anyway, I'm in a very bad mood about the whole business. I feel even grumpier than usual.'

Horace chuckled. 'That's the spirit, Gus! Your glumness will be powerful enough to infect the party and make everyone as miserable as you are!'

Horace grinned at the girls. 'Making mischief is such fun, and now my evil work is done.'

With a nod of his wobbly head to bid them farewell, Horace frolicked his way out of the stables, his mean-spirited laughter ringing in their ears.

'It seems that Horace has got us this time, Livvy,' Eliza said. 'And the duchess will be furious when our pony turns up without a costume.'

'Hang on a minute!' Olivia perked up. 'I think I've got an idea. There's an outfit in my dressing-up chest that might just help save the day!'

'A costume? One that *you* used to wear? But will it fit Gus?' Eliza didn't look convinced.

'No,' Olivia agreed, 'but it will fit *me*! I'm going to grab it; Eliza, wait here and I'll be back in a flash!'

'Where is she?' Eliza paced the stables anxiously, talking aloud to herself. 'It's been positively ages . . . we're going to be late for the party!'

'Here I am!' The voice belonged to Olivia, but the shape that walked back in through the front door was not a girl at all . . . but a carrot.

A giant carrot – bright orange with a green top sprouting out of its foam-rubber head where the hair should be, holes for Olivia's eyes, and her arms and legs sticking out of the sides.

'Livvy?' Eliza said. 'Is that you in there?'

'Yes!' The green top of the

carrot head bobbled about in an excited fashion. 'It's me! Isn't it super? This was my Halloween costume last year and then I thought what could possibly be better to cheer up small children at a party than being led about on a pony by a giant carrot?'

'Well, I suppose it might cheer them up,' Eliza admitted, 'although children don't really like carrots, do they?'

'No, of course they don't,' Olivia agreed, 'but ponies love carrots – that's the whole point!'

'I don't love carrots.'

It was Gus. He'd stuck his head out over the door of his stall and was looking more gloomy than ever – if that was even possible – at the sight of Olivia!

'That's all you ever hear about, isn't it?' Gus sighed. **'Oooh, ponies love carrots! So do rabbits! Talk to a rabbit and it's all yum, yum, yum, carrots for supper!'** He pulled a face. **'Not me,**

though! I don't give a fig for a carrot. A totally overrated vegetable, if you ask me.'

'Wow!' Olivia shook her head in disbelief. 'You're capable of being negative about absolutely anything, aren't you, Gus?'

'What can I say?' Gus shrugged. 'I'm a trough-half-empty kind of horse.'

Olivia sighed and handed a change of clothes to Eliza. 'Here, I brought you something to wear too – from my own wardrobe, though, not the dressing-up box.'

'Oooh, super!' Eliza was delighted as she put the outfit on. 'I love your clothes, Livvy! Much more practical than my white nightie.'

'Right, then!' Olivia said. 'We're all set to go. Gus, what do you say? Shall we go to the party?'

'All right,' Gus sighed, 'I'll go, but—'

'Yes, yes, Gus, we know,' the girls chorused.

'You won't like it!'

Olivia and Eliza led Gus back into the stall and, a moment later, the enchanted mist began to rise.

'**Oh, honestly!**' Gus grizzled. '**I really will have to see a doctor if this damp mist keeps rising up every time we go somewhere! I've got sinus problems too, you know, and—**'

'Gus!' Olivia scolded. 'If you don't try to look on the bright side, we'll never be able to break the spell and you'll be stuck like this forever! Think cheery thoughts of wonderful things like rainbows and fluffy white kittens and yummy sweets and all the best foods in the world – popcorn and real fruit ice cream and candyfloss and sugar cakes and fairy lights and fireworks and sparkly—'

'Wowsers!' Eliza said. 'Livvy, it's like magic – how did you do that?'

It was indeed like magic because, just as Olivia was

listing all the best things in the world, the mist cleared and the girls and Gus found themselves standing on the lawn of a most beautiful country estate.

In front of them, a party was already in full swing, with all of the very wonderful things Olivia had just mentioned, and much more besides!

Along with the fluffy white kittens – who were doing acrobatics on the lawn – there were dancing dachshunds doing backflips. Velvety-red butterflies filled the skies and flew in formation to make love hearts in mid-air. There was even a real castle that turned out to be bouncy on the inside.

'It's like a wonderland!' Olivia breathed.

'Why, thank you!' The duchess appeared beside them. 'Never let it be said that the Duchess of Derryshire doesn't know how to throw a party! I must say it's about time you got here, though – we've all been waiting.'

'What's that massive queue over there for?' Olivia asked.

'That,' the duchess replied, 'is the queue for the pony rides.'

Gus groaned. **'Everybody wants to ride on me? Just my rotten luck!'**

'Come on, Gus, you'll love it!' Olivia said. 'Just think how happy it will make you, knowing that you've brought such enjoyment to all these children. Besides, you might even have fun yourself!'

'I can guarantee that I won't,' Gus replied. His

ears were flat back and now Olivia felt the glumness creeping up on her as well. Gus was as grumpy as ever, and if they couldn't somehow break his curse, the rest of the Spellbound ponies were doomed.

Chapter Six

The children all cheered at the sight of the giant carrot leading the handsome bay pony towards them.

'Hooray! Pony rides at last!' a sweet-faced girl at the front of the queue shouted out with excitement.

'Oww!' Gus grumbled. 'Keep the noise down, please! Look at the size of my ears here – there's clearly no need to shout at me!'

'I'm sure she didn't mean to hurt your ears, Gus,' the duchess said. 'This is Jemima and she's just so thrilled you're here at last, aren't you, Jemima?'

'Oooh, yes!' Jemima bounced up and down. 'Why, all I've ever wanted my whole life was to ride a pony and—'

'Yes, yes, you can stop with the blibber-blabber,' Gus grumbled. **'Climb on, Jemima, you noisy monster, and let's get this over with, shall we?'**

Jemima's face fell a little but she climbed bravely up on to the mounting block and Olivia helped her to put her foot in the stirrup and clamber on board.

'Ooh, thank you, kind carrot,' Jemima said. 'You're my very favourite vegetable!'

'Well, would you look at that!' Eliza said.

'A child who likes carrots!'

Jemima sat up straight in the saddle. 'How do I make him go?' she asked Olivia.

'Give him a tap with your heels,' Olivia suggested.

Jemima gave Gus a gentle nudge. 'Come on, pony!' she cooed.

'Humph!' Gus put his ears back. **'How dare you poke me in the ribs! What an amateur you are! I've had some twits on my back before, Jemima, but you, you unfortunate child, really take the cake! Sitting up there as pointless as a pork chop! Oh, I do wish you'd never got on board. What will it take to make you climb straight back off again?'**

Jemima's cheeks flushed hot pink with embarrassment and her bottom lip began to tremble, tears forming in her eyes.

'Why isn't the pony ride happening? What's

going on?' The queue of children began to grow restless.

'Make him go, Jemima!' one boy shouted.

'Yes!' they all chorused. 'Come on, Jemima!'

Olivia, meanwhile, was tugging at Gus's bridle. 'Gus, come on! If you don't give the children rides, we'll never break the witch's spell. Try to be kind,' she pleaded, 'and less grumpy.'

'Oh, give it a rest, Livvy!' Gus turned on Olivia with his ears flat back. **'You're only making me more miserable with your whining,'** he grizzled.

'Go, Gus! Go, Gus!' the children chorused.

'I want to get off!' Jemima was bawling now. **'Well, get off, then, sobby-pants!'** Gus grumped. **'Can someone fetch a towel? I'm all damp from her splishy tears. Ick!'**

'Oh, good grief.' Olivia shook her head in disbelief as a defeated Jemima climbed down.

'Come on, then, who's up for it?' Gus snorted. **'All aboard the Misery Express! Toot toot!'**

'Ohhh, I'm next!' A girl who introduced herself as Violet leaped forward and scrambled straight up on to the mounting block and eagerly on to Gus's back.

'Steady on there, Edmund Hillary!' Gus griped. 'You're not climbing Everest, you know. I'm a pony, not a mountain. You need to be a bit more graceful – clambering all over me like a clod-footed lump!'

'That's *enough*, Gus!' Olivia scolded.

'Wahhh! I want to get down too.' Violet began to sob. 'He's too grumpy.'

'Ha!' Gus gloated. 'I got rid of that one even quicker than the one before!'

'Look,' Eliza said, 'the children are all leaving!'

Sure enough, the queue of riders was shrinking right before their eyes.

'I'm not getting on Grumpy Gus,' one girl said, quivering as she gave up and headed for the candyfloss stand.

'Me neither,' another agreed. 'I'm going to

ride on the merry-go-round instead.'

'No, please, he'll be better next time, truly.'
Olivia tried to stop them all from leaving.

'But will he really?' One of the girls still in the
queue looked anxious. 'He seems to be getting even
grumpier.'

'Yes, look – he's still got his ears back,' another
girl pointed out, 'and his tail is swishing like mad!'

It was true. Gus was snarling with his ears
flattened to his skull and his tail whirling about
like crazy. He had his teeth bared in a grimace as
he thrashed about like a shark in a tank.

'Do you see what's happening here?' Eliza said to Olivia. 'Is it my imagination or is he getting worse?'

'It's the curse,' Olivia said. 'Every time a child tells Gus that he's beastly, it seems to make the witch's spell more powerful! He's getting grumpier by the minute – we're losing him!'

'Who's next, then?' Gus bellowed.

'Not me!' the children shrieked in unison.

'Oh no.' Olivia felt her heart sink. 'We're doomed. The witch has won.'

Then, from the queue, a hand shot up.

'I'll ride him,' a timid wee voice spoke out.

All heads turned and there stood a girl with sweet dark curls, wearing a pearl tiara.

'Ooooh, goodness!' the crowd cried.

For the hand that had shot up belonged to none other than one of the birthday girls: Lady Patience, daughter of the Duchess of Derryshire.

81

Chapter Seven

As Gus griped and thrashed, teensy Lady Patience stepped up to the mounting block.

'I would like a ride, please,' Patience said.

'Are you sure, dearest child?' the duchess asked. 'He's such a grumpy pony.'

'Very grumpy,' Gus confirmed.

'I think he looks adorable,' Lady Patience said, smiling.

'And such fun! I love a pony with spirit!'

'Spirit?' Eliza boggled. 'Mean spirit, more like.'

'Shhhh,' Olivia hissed. 'Let's not put her off! Lady Patience is possibly our only hope.'

Lady Patience, meanwhile, had already climbed up on to the block and now she was adjusting her skirts, preparing to mount.

'Shall we go for a ride, my darling boy?' she said to Gus.

'Who are you calling darling?' Gus grumped.

Patience giggled. 'Oh, you are a funny pony!' She flung herself on board and grabbed the reins. 'Off we go, then! Let's have an adventure. We can go round the lake – there's a lovely bridle path.'

'Ugh,' Gus groaned. **'Just my rotten luck that you want to go to such an awful place. It's full of swans and butterflies, you know. Dreadful!'**

'Ha ha ha!' Lady Patience laughed. 'Oh,

stop it – you're too funny!'

'**Stop saying that!**' Gus swished his tail and put his ears flat back. '**I'm not funny at all. I'm a nasty black storm cloud of misery!**'

Lady Patience gave him a hearty pat on his neck. 'Nonsense!' she cooed. 'You seem like a very nice pony to me. Why, I'll wager you have the most marvellous trot. Shall we see?'

'**Hmmmm, very well, then,**' Gus said grudgingly. '**I'll trot for you. But I won't like it.**'

Before Olivia and Eliza knew what was happening, Gus had trotted off with Lady Patience on his back and was speeding across the lawn towards the lake.

'Gosh,' Eliza said, 'will you look at that!'

'He does have quite a spectacular trot!' Olivia said. 'Who knew?'

'He's going a long way away.' The Duchess of

Derryshire looked anxious. 'He will bring my darling Patience back again, won't he?'

Meanwhile, out on the bridle path, Lady Patience was in no hurry to go home.

'What a lovely time I'm having with you, Gus!' she giggled.

'I bet you're not really!' Gus grumbled. **'People very seldom have a good time when they're with me.'**

'I'm sure that's not true.' Lady Patience gave him a sweet stroke on his glossy bay neck. 'I'm quite certain you have a lovely canter. Will you do a canter for me, Gus?'

'All right,' Gus said, **'but I won't like it.'**

'Look at him.' Eliza was amazed. 'He's cantering!'

'And his ears are pricked forward,' said Olivia, observing the scene.

'Oh dear!' The Duchess of Derryshire still
looked worried. 'Do you hear that? I think Patience
is crying out in fear!'

'No, no, no,' Olivia said. 'She's laughing!'

It was true. Lady Patience was whooping with joy as they cantered all the way round the lake, and she was still laughing as Gus swooped back to return once more to the front of the queue.

'That was amazing,' she giggled as she leapt down. 'What a fun pony!'

'Oh, me next!' It was Lady Patience's twin sister, Lady Lilibeth.

Before anyone could stop her, Lilibeth was on board.

'**Crikey,**' Gus grumbled, '**you Derryshire girls are like buses. You all come at once!**'

'Ha ha!' Lady Lilibeth laughed. 'Oh, you're right, Patience. He is a hoot, isn't he?'

'I told you so,' Lady Patience agreed. 'He acts grumpy but he doesn't mean it, really.'

'You know what I think?' Lady Lilibeth said to Gus. 'I think your bark is worse than your bite.'

'Oh no.' Gus shook his head. **'My bite is really quite bad.'**

'Ha ha ha!' Lady Lilibeth was in stitches. 'Too funny! Come on, Gus, let's go round the lake. Off we trot!'

'All right,' Gus complained, **'but this time I really won't like it.'**

Off he trotted, and by the time he returned again with Lady Lilibeth beaming, Gus had his ears pricked forward and there was a sparkle in his eye.

'What fun that was, Gus!' Lady Lilibeth said. 'You're the best pony in the whole world.'

Lady Patience agreed.

'Oh, you're just saying that,' Gus grumbled.

'No, we're truly not,' the girls chorused. 'We love you, Gus!'

With that, both of the twins threw themselves

at the Spellbound pony, wrapped their arms round his neck and gave him the most massive hug.

'**Eeek!**' Gus squeaked. '**What are you doing?**'

'Giving you cuddles, you silly pony!' the girls laughed.

'**Ooooh,**' Gus said. '**I've never felt like this before but . . . I . . . I think . . . I think I like it!**'

'Crikey!' Eliza said. 'Look at him, Livvy. Why is he quivering like that . . . and what is that funny noise that he's making?'

Livvy stared at Gus. 'If I didn't know better,' she said, 'I'd say he was . . . laughing!'

'Ho ho ho!' Gus was guffawing now. His sides were heaving in and out like bagpipes with the merriment of it all. **'Oh, you girls do make me laugh!'**

Then suddenly Gus's laughter ceased.

'That's odd,' Gus said. **'I've come over all strange and tingly. Oh goodness! What's happening to me? I feel quite peculiar!'**

'He does look very odd,' the duchess agreed. 'Do you see how he's gone all gold and shimmery?'

'Yes!' Olivia said. 'It's as if the light of a thousand suns is glowing inside him.'

 90

The duchess frowned. 'I mean, is this a part of the pony-ride package, because I'm not paying extra . . .'

'No, Duchess,' Olivia said, 'don't you see? Something very magical is happening to Gus.'

'Oh yes, Livvy!' Eliza squeaked. 'Of course! It's the witch's curse – it's been broken! The hug must have done it. Gus is transforming!'

'I'm transforming, you say?' Gus said. **'Well, all right but I won't like—'**

But before Gus could say anything more, he had lost the power to speak and began whinnying instead!

Olivia whooped with joy. 'The spell! It's been broken!'

Gus was a real pony once more.

Chapter Eight

That afternoon, Gus was in fearfully good humour as he gave every single child in the queue a pony ride round the lake.

'He really is a marvellous pony now,' Eliza enthused. 'Look at him! He's got his ears pricked forward and he looks so happy in his work.'

'To think all it took to cure his case of the grumps was a little bit of love and some hugs!' Olivia giggled.

'Girls!'

It was the Duchess of Derryshire and she did not look happy at all.

'I have something serious to discuss with you,' the duchess said. 'I've just found this hidden away underneath the candyfloss stall.'

The duchess held out what looked like a shredded rainbow.

'Oh no!' Eliza whispered to Olivia. 'Gus's costume! She'll be furious when we tell her that Horace destroyed it.'

'What is the meaning of this?' the duchess demanded. 'Is that why he wasn't wearing it? Because you had damaged it? Is this some sort of prank, because it has made me quite grumpy. Please explain yourselves!'

'Uh, oh, you see it's not our fault, your duchessness,' Olivia mumbled as she tried to find excuses. Then a thought struck her like a lightning bolt. 'It's actually a very brilliant idea to add to the party fun!'

'Is it?' The duchess frowned. 'How so?'

'Well,' Olivia explained, 'Gus pointed out that it didn't seem entirely fair that it's just the birthday

95

girls who get all the presents. So we've come up with a solution.'

'Have we?' Eliza was baffled. 'When did that happen?'

'Shush, Eliza,' Olivia whispered. 'Just play along. I've got a plan.'

'May I have the suit and a pair of scissors, please?' Olivia said.

The duchess sighed. 'Very well, I suppose the costume is ruined now anyway, so I'll give you the chance to fix things. But I can't imagine what you're going to do. Look at it – it's in ribbons!'

'Exactly!' Olivia said.

She got to work with the scissors, chopping the ribbons into long lengths of rainbow silk. And then she spread out a picnic blanket and set up a sign on the lawn.

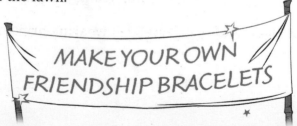

MAKE YOUR OWN
FRIENDSHIP BRACELETS

'You see,' she explained to Eliza as she braided three of the ribbons together, then measured them round her own wrist, bound the ends and tied them off. 'We'll use the ribbons so that all the kids at the party can make their own bracelets, and then each of them will have something to take home as a gift.'

'Ohhhh, that looks amazing!' Eliza admired the rainbow bracelet that Olivia had made for herself.

'Oh, I say! Did you make this? It looks like super fun!'

It was Lady Lilibeth. She plonked herself down on the blankets, grabbed a handful of ribbons and began to braid herself a bracelet. Within minutes, Lady Patience was making one too. Soon the entire birthday party had joined them and everyone was wearing armfuls of rainbow friendship bracelets.

'It's the perfect end to the perfect party!' Eliza said.

'Not quite the end,' the duchess replied. 'There's still the birthday cake to be cut and all the special desserts to be eaten: raspberries and ice cream,

cherries and cream, and meringues and lollies and all kinds of yummy toppings. You girls absolutely must not leave without having something to eat too. This has been the best party ever, thanks to you and your adorable, cheerful pony!'

MAKE YOUR OWN
FRIENDSHIP BRACELETS

That evening, Olivia sat at the dinner table with her stomach groaning from eating too much party food.

'Are you all right?' Mrs Campbell asked. 'You've barely touched your dinner.'

'I'm fine, Mum, honest,' Olivia said.

Mrs Campbell began to clear the table. 'Can you girls help me with the dishes, please? Olivia, you can wash this time and Ella, you can dry.'

'It's not fair!' Ella grumped. 'Why do I have to dry? Just my rotten luck!'

Olivia giggled.

'What are you laughing at, squirt?' Ella snapped.

'What you said – *just my rotten luck*!' Olivia giggled again. 'I have a friend who's always saying that.'

'Humph!' Ella grumped. 'I find it hard to believe you even have any friends at all – you're so annoying!'

'Oh dear, you're extra grumpy tonight, Ella,' Mrs Campbell observed.

'Yes, she is,' Olivia gasped. 'But it's okay, Mum. I know how to fix it!'

'Yikes!' Ella let out a squeak. 'Hey! What are you doing, twerp! Quit it!'

But Olivia would not quit. She had Ella in her arms and she was giving her the most massive hug.

'Trust me, I've seen this work. It's the best way to cure the grumps!' Olivia said as she hugged her big sister.

'You're bonkers!' Ella replied. But she had a smile on her face now, and then she began to giggle. 'Okay, okay, Olivia. You've cured me. You can let go now!'

101

Olivia released her sister from the hug and Ella looked at her and smiled. 'You really are quite silly and funny, aren't you?' she said.

'That's me,' Olivia agreed.

Ella gave her a quick hug in return and picked up the tea towel. 'Come on, then, twerp, let's go and do the dishes.'

'Oh, wait!' Olivia said. 'I almost forgot. I made a present for you.'

She fished around and pulled something shiny out of her pocket.

'What's that?' Ella asked.

'It's a rainbow friendship bracelet,' Olivia said.

'You're not my friend, you know.' Ella sniffed grumpily. 'You're just my stinky little sister.'

All the same, Ella tied it round her wrist and Olivia saw her staring admiringly at it.

The next day, when they were leaving for school, Olivia noticed that her big sister was much more cheerful than she usually was in the morning, and when she looked at Ella's wrist, she was still wearing the bracelet.

Chapter Nine

That afternoon on the way home from school Olivia called in at Pemberley Stables. The locked stable doors slid magically open at her touch and she walked inside.

As she moved through the corridor, a soft nicker and the sound of hoofbeats on straw could be heard in the stalls, and soon five heads appeared over the bottom half of the stall doors.

'Hello, my beautiful ponies,' Olivia said as the five ponies eagerly lifted their heads to the sound of her voice.

'Darling Bess.' She stroked the soft muzzle of the elegant black mare. Bess was the first pony the girls had unbound, convincing the naughty mare to give up her life of highway robbery. Bess gave her tail a playful swish and Olivia giggled. 'Good to see you behaving yourself!'

Looking handsome in his stall was Prince, a sleek dapple-grey racehorse who'd been cursed with a greedy fondness for scoffing cream buns that sapped his speed. The girls had fixed this problem too. 'Now you're fit and ready to race.' Olivia gave him a pat on his glossy neck.

The next horse she greeted was a snow-white mare with a mane that was so fine and shimmery it was as if it had been spun from pure silk. 'Pretty as a princess, my brilliant Sparkle,' Olivia cooed as she put a braid into the pony's silken forelock.

'And you, Champ,' she said to the palomino stamping and demanding attention in another stall. 'We must go showjumping soon, my clever superstar.'

Champ looked pleased with that and Olivia was about to say more, when her attention was drawn to the latest addition to the stables. A handsome dark bay head was at the stall door. He had his ears pricked forward, keen and happy.

'Gus!' Olivia was delighted to see him in such a good mood. 'Oh, welcome to the stables – a real pony like the others at last!' Without hesitating she threw her arms round him and gave him a massive hug.

'He's fitting in so well, isn't he?' a voice from behind Olivia piped up. 'He seems very happy to be here. In fact, he's the happiest pony in the stables. It's hard to believe he was ever grumpy!'

'Eek!' Olivia jumped and spun round to see Eliza behind her. 'I wish you wouldn't sneak up on me like that!'

'Sorry,' Eliza giggled, 'but it is one of the side effects of having a ghost for a best friend.'

'I suppose it is,' Olivia agreed.

'Did you notice what Gus is wearing round his neck?' Eliza asked.

107

Olivia looked again and noticed that Gus had a necklace made from rainbow ribbons.

'The twins made it for him –' Eliza smiled – 'to say thank you for being such a super birthday boy; isn't that right, Gus?'

Gus nickered with delight as the girls oohed and aahed over his necklace. They were so absorbed in their admiration that they failed to notice a spooky mist rolling in through the front door of the stables. Now the mist was beginning to rise . . . and through the foggy air came the haunting bay of ghostly dogs.

'Do you hear that?' Eliza shivered.

A moment later a dark silhouette loomed in through the stable door. The apparition floated above the mist, drawing closer to the girls, until at last Lady Luella, the mistress of Pemberley Manor, stood before them.

She was very beautiful in an eerie sort of way.
She wore a black velvet hunting jacket and a
hunting skirt, the sort you'd wear to ride side-
saddle. Her hair tumbled over her shoulders in
lush auburn waves and her skin
was alabaster, like Eliza's. She
had flashing emerald eyes
and imperious arched
brows that she raised
now at the sight of
the girls standing
before her.

'I heard from the
duchess that you girls
have been busy,' she
said. 'Now I see it's
true. You've managed
to unbind another pony.'

'Yes,' Eliza said. 'This is Gus. He was cursed to be grumpy but he's not any more.'

'So you see,' Olivia added, 'the curse is almost broken.'

Lady Luella arched a questioning brow. 'You think you've beaten the witch, Olivia? Not yet, child. It's true you have done well . . . and the spell does say that *two brave girls may turn the tables.* But there is more work to be done before the dark magic can be defeated and, as you know, I cannot help you. The spell was cast at my bidding but it is beyond my power to control it. The task ahead rests on your shoulders and it will not be easy, I'm afraid. The witch is very powerful.'

'We're ready,' Eliza said. 'Livvy and I, together, are going to free them all!'

'Is that so?' Lady Luella hovered high above the mist. 'Eliza, you know magic is a tricky business.

Your friend Olivia must be careful. What you wish for is not always what you want. Heaven knows, when I wished this spell upon the stables, I never knew I would lose you, Eliza. I wish you would come home.'

'I'll come home, Mama,' Eliza said, 'when all the poor ponies are set free.'

'Very well,' Lady Luella said. 'Five spells you've broken now – the others still remain. Farewell, Eliza, dear heart, until we meet again.'

With a wistful look at her daughter, Lady Luella departed in a swirl of mist.

'Gosh, it's chilly in here when she visits!' Olivia shivered. 'You can really feel the magic in the stables tonight.'

'Look!' Eliza exclaimed. 'The sixth stall. The name plaque is glowing!'

'The new pony,' Olivia whispered. 'It can't be!'

'But it is,' Eliza whispered back.

Sure enough, there was a name already glowing on the plaque of the next stable door.

Eliza clapped her hands with glee. 'The next Spellbound pony is here!'

NEXT IN THE SERIES . . .

Dancing and Dreams

Margot looked up at the girls through her long lashes. 'Really?' she said softly. 'Me? Clumsy? I mean, I'm not one to argue. In fact, I never argue with anyone and rarely say boo to a ghost. I never like to give an opinion – I hardly dare speak up. All the same – me, clumsy? It can't possibly be true!'

'And why is that, Margot?' Olivia asked.

Margot bit her lip and looked down at her hooves for a long time as if she didn't want to speak, but then at last she blurted out, 'Because I love to dance! I want to be a *famous* dancer, in *fact*. And I can't be a dance-sensation if I'm cursed to be a clumsy clot!'

'Oh, poor, poor pony!' Eliza looked like she might cry. 'That witch really is a wretch! Imagine cursing Margot to be clumsy.'

'We will help you, Margot, I promise,' Olivia said. 'Let's begin by getting you on your feet again.' She took hold of Margot's halter and tried to pull her up but the grey pony managed to slip loose of her halter entirely so that Olivia fell back and banged into the water trough.

'Owww!'

'Gosh, you're quite clumsy too, aren't you?' Eliza pointed out.

'The halter slipped,' Olivia groaned.

'Are you all right?' Eliza asked.

'I'm fine.' Olivia rubbed her sore elbow. 'I whacked myself on the water trough. It's quite cramped in here . . .'

'That's it!' Eliza exclaimed. 'This stall is hardly helping matters. It's very small. We need somewhere bigger so that Margot can dance properly and get in some practice.'

'I suppose that might help,' Olivia agreed, 'but where could we go?'

'Ohhh!' Eliza's brilliant green eyes blazed brightly. 'I know just the place. It's a very grand ballroom – I danced there myself back in the day!'

'A grand ballroom?' Margot looked very worried. 'Will there be lots of people there? I'm not very good with lots of people. All those introductions and having to say hello. Besides, ummm, I have nothing to wear!'

'Yes, you do!' Eliza pointed to the rack of ballet tutus at the back of the stall.

'Where did that clothing rack appear *from?*' Margot wondered out loud as Olivia bounded over to look through the clothes.

'Ohhhh, the cherry-red tutu!' Eliza squeaked with delight. 'Pull that one out, Livvy! It would look gorgeous on a grey pony!'

'It's a bit bright, isn't it?' Margot said. 'I don't really like to draw attention to myself. I usually like to wear colours that make me blend into the walls.'

'Oh, surely not!' Eliza giggled. 'Silly pony! You'll look lovely in this. Let's put it on now.'

Olivia helped the pony into her tutu.

'It looks very good on you, Margot,' Olivia said.

Margot blushed. 'I'm not used to so much attention,' she said softly. 'I'm very shy and—'

120

'Look!' Eliza pointed to the straw on the floor of the stall. 'Enchanted mist! This is it – we're on our way!'

'On our way where, exactly?' Olivia asked. 'Eliza, you never explained where it is that we are going . . .'

To be continued . . .

TAKE A SNEAK PEAK AT WHERE THE
SPELLBOUND PONIES' STORY ALL BEGAN . . .

Magic and Mischief

It was like Christmas. No, better than that – it was like every single Christmas *ever* all at once! Olivia had hardly been able to sleep last night, after her mother had said they could have riding lessons. Now, as the car turned down the lane and the stables lay up ahead, she gave a strangled squeak.

'Ha ha!' Ella piped up from the back seat. 'Livvy sounds like a meerkat!'

'Ella, don't be horrid to your little sister,' said Mrs Campbell.

Ella snorted. 'You've already moved us to the middle of nowhere *and* taken away my mobile phone. How much more can you punish me?'

'You'll grow horns if you use your phone too much,' Mrs Campbell replied. 'I read it in the paper. Children are sprouting them on the back of their heads from spending all day on their devices. And that, Ella, is exactly why we moved here. There's no need to be glued to your screen when you have all this countryside to play in and such lovely fresh air!'

Mrs Campbell said the word *devices* as if they were poison and *fresh air* as if she was about to burst into song.

'I don't know why I had to come today.' Ella continued her grumbling from the back seat. 'I don't even like horses!' But up front Olivia wasn't paying her big sister the slightest bit of attention. She was utterly transfixed by the stone buildings covered in ivy up ahead and the sign above them that read:

PEMBERLEY STABLES

'Do you think we should have phoned ahead back when we were in Pemberley village? What if all the horses are busy?' she asked.

'I tried the stables' number, but there was no answer,' her mum replied. 'If they're too booked up to give you a lesson right now, we can always make arrangements to come back.' . . .

To be continued . . .

Out Now

CAN THEY SAVE THEM ALL?

Spellbound
Ponies
Wishes and
Weddings

STACY GREGG

Out Now

CAN THEY SAVE THEM ALL?

Spellbound
Ponies
Sugar and
Spice

STACY GREGG

Out Now

CAN THEY SAVE THEM ALL?

Spellbound
Ponies
Magic and
Mischief

STACY GREGG

Collect